WHO *IS* GERONIMO STILTON?

by Samantha Tattletail and Simon Squealer

Geronimo Stilton: What's he really like?

His books sell millions of copies, and his newspaper, *The Rodent's Gazette,* is the bestselling paper in New Mouse City. He's well known in the tropics and at the North Pole, on the highest mountain and across oceans, in the countryside and in the city. . . .

But does anyone know the *real* Geronimo Stilton?

We're all curious about his **HIDDEN SIDE**, his **PRIVATE LIFE**, and all the little things this famous mouse loves. Timid and shy by nature, *Geronimo Stilton* is, by all accounts, a true gentlemouse. But even he has flaws: some **small**, some

enormouse!

And we, **Samantha Tattletail** and Simon Squealer, will give you the whole scoop. We've discovered Geronimo Stilton's biggest **SECRETS** through our exclusive interviews!

It's not easy to track down this information, but together with our talented photographer **RED PAPARATZ**, we've done it!

We'll tell you ...
...everything

RED PAPARATZ

THE SECRET WORLD OF
Geronimo Stilton

by Samantha Tattletail
and Simon Squealer

Scholastic Inc.

ISBN 978-0-545-48254-7

Based on an original idea by Elisabetta Dami.
www.geronimostilton.com

Published by Scholastic Inc., 557 Broadway, New York, NY 10012.
SCHOLASTIC and associated logos are trademarks and/or registered trademarks of Scholastic Inc.

Stilton is the name of a famous English cheese. It is a registered trademark of the Stilton Cheese Makers' Association. For more information, go to www.stiltoncheese.com.

Text by Samantha Tattletail and Simon Squealer
Original title *La vera storia di Geronimo Stilton*
Cover by Giuseppe Ferrario
Illustrations by Silvia Bigolin, Lorenzo Chiavini, Vinicio Corda, Michele Dallorso, Maria Defilippo, Umberto Fizialetti, Mirella Monesi, Blasco Pisapia, Roberto Ronchi, and Stefano Scagni
Graphics by Merenguita Gingermouse and Zeppola Zap

Translated by and special thanks to Emily Clement
Interior design by Becky James

12 11 10 9 8 7 6 5 4 3 2 1   12 13 14 15 16 17/0

Printed in the U.S.A.   40
First printing, September 2012

THE BEGINNING

by Samantha Tattletail

Nobody knows where *Geronimo Stilton* really comes from.

His birth date is **TOP SECRET**, and nobody knows who his true parents are!

But we do know a few things about the early years of his life. . . .

It All Started Just Like This . . .

by Samantha Tattletail

Geronimo Stilton's cousin Trap was one of his very first playmates. But these two didn't always get along, as you can see in the photo below!

We asked Mrs. Sweetie Softpaws, his kindergarten teacher, what Geronimo was like.

Sweetie: Geronimo? Oh, he was so sweet.

Samantha: And tell us, did Geronimo and his cousin Trap always play well together?

Little Geronimo

Little Trap

Sweetie: No, no, no. Trap was always playing tricks on him!

Samantha: Really? Like what?

Sweetie: Oh, one time he put a live frog in Geronimo's underwear.

Samantha: How absurd!

Sweetie: Another time, he smeared all the pages in Geronimo's journal with jam. And once he hid  his glasses in a bowl of soup. And another time he tied a knot in his tail! But Geronimo never got angry. When he was little, he was just as gentle as he is now!

It's not worth getting angry!

NOTES FROM AN INTERVIEW
WITH TRAP

"I've always done everything for Geronimo. In school, I always let him do my homework, and I never even took a peek to make sure the answers were **RIGHT**!"

Now *that's* what I call trust!

Trap Stilton,
Geronimo's cousin

CHATTER

Super Scoop!

They say that the editor of The Rodent's Gazette is funny, but that he doesn't have a sense of humor!

Cousin Trap just played a joke on Geronimo: He put a spider in his desk drawer. We caught Geronimo screaming at the top of his lungs. What happened to his sense of humor?!

CAN IT BE TRUE?

HIS ADVENTUROUS SISTER, THEA

by Simon Squealer

Just for you, we've interviewed Thea Stilton, Geronimo Stilton's sister. It wasn't easy to catch up with her, since she was participating in a motorcycle race in the Mousehara Desert, and cell phones don't really work there.

Thea Stilton

SIMON: Hello? **Hello? Hello?** Can you hear me, Miss Stilton?

THEA: Loud and clear . . . **Bzzzz** . . . But in a little bit . . . **Bzzz** . . . in the desert . . . **Bzzz** . . .

SIMON: I'll try to be quick. What can you tell us about your brother, Geronimo?

Simon Squealer

THEA: Geronimo? . . . **Bzzz** . . . I love my brother . . . . **Bzzz** . . .

Simon: Of course, of course, but surely something about him must bug you.

THEA: **Bzzz** . . . Well, he's a **terrible** driver.

Simon: Really?!

THEA: Yes, unfortunately . . . **Bzzz** . . .

So I usually drive him places. . . . **Bzzz** . . . But he's always complaining. . . . **Bzzz** . . .

Simon: Complaining? Why?

THEA: He says . . . **Bzzz** . . .

Simon: What? Can you repeat that?

THEA: **Bzzz** . . . **Bzzz** . . .

Simon: Hello? Hello? **Hello?** Miss Stilton?! I can't hear anything!

THEA: *HE SAYS THAT I DRIVE TOO FAST!*

Simon: Oh, I see. And is that true?

THEA: No, absolutely . . . **Bzzz** . . . and he's such a scaredy-mouse! **Bzzz** . . . **Bzzz** . . .

Then the line went dead.

CHATTER

Super Scoop!

The editor of The Rodent's Gazette likes rock music!

We caught Geronimo at a rock concert. He was even wearing a leather jacket! He claimed his assistant Pinky Pick dragged him to the show, but we don't believe it. Do you?

CAN IT BE TRUE?

HIS GRANDFATHER WILLIAM SHORTPAWS

by Simon Squealer

We've contacted Geronimo's grandfather **Mr. William Shortpaws**. He's a very important rodent, and the founder of *The Rodent's Gazette*.

Simon: Hello? Mr. Shortpaws? I'm hoping for a short interv—

William Shortpaws: Interview? Well, come on, let's get going, I don't have much time! *I HAVE WORK TO DO! I'M VERY BUSY!*

Simon: Um, I'll try to hurr—

William Shortpaws: Faster! Hurry up!

Simon: Um, well, I wanted to know . . .

William Shortpaws: Go! Go! Go!

Simon: As I was saying . . .

William Shortpaws: Well, what are you waiting for? Did you fall asleep? Come on, I'm in a rush! *I HAVE WORK TO DO! I'M VERY BUSY!* Why am I wasting my time here?!

13

Simon: Actually, I . . .

William Shortpaws: Well, what about this interview? I'm waiting!

Simon: So, what do you think of your grandson—

William Shortpaws: Too late! I have to get off the phone, I have things to do! *I HAVE WORK TO DO! I'M VERY BUSY!*

Then he hung up on me! What a strange rodent!

GO, GO, GO!

I HAVE WORK TO DO!

I'M VERY BUSY!

William Shortpaws

HIS DEAR NEPHEW BENJAMIN

by Samantha Tattletail

Benjamin is Geronimo's favorite nephew, and he was very excited to talk about Geronimo.

"Uncle Geronimo is an **EXCEPTIONAL** rodent! Even when he is very **BUSY**, he always finds time to **PLAY** with me!"

But even Benjamin has his little secrets. . . .

Did you know that he has a **BAD GRADE** on his report card?! It's true! He failed physical education, just like his uncle Geronimo!

Nice move, Benjamin!

HIS GOLDFISH, HANNIBAL

by Simon Squealer

We snuck into Geronimo's house for just a few minutes and were able to interview his pet goldfish, **Hannibal**.

Simon: Since you obviously know him well, what are Geronimo Stilton's favorite foods?

Hannibal: BLUB . . . BLUB . . . BLUB . . .

Simon: Amaaaaaazing!

Hannibal: BLUB . . . BLUB . . . BLUB . . .

Simon: With chopped nuts and Gorgonzola melted on top? Amaaaaaazing! **What else? What else?**

Hannibal: BLUB . . . BLUB . . . BLUB . . .

Simon: But does he like his provolone sliced, cubed, or grated?

Hannibal: BLUB . . . BLUB . . . BLUB . . .

Simon: Amaaaaaazing! **What else? What else?**

Hannibal: BLUB . . . BLUB . . . BLUB . . .

Simon: And he stuffs it with fontina and

DEEP-FRIES it??? Amaaaaazing!

Hannibal: BLUB ... BLUB ... BLUB ...

Simon: Amaaaaazing! I can see that Stilton is a real food lover!!!

I love you, Hannibal!

GERONIMO STILTON, WORLD TRAVELER

by Samantha Tattletail

He's always getting sick!

Even though he's often forced to travel for work, Geronimo Stilton isn't a very good **traveler**.

seasick . . .

HIS OFFICE

by Samantha Tattletail
and Simon Squealer

We've infiltrated the offices of *The Rodent's Gazette* at 17 Swiss Cheese Center, where *Geronimo Stilton* works. Fortunately, he wasn't there at the time — probably because we were there in the middle of the **NIGHT**.

We found many interesting clues about him in his office!

The walls were covered with **newspaper articles** that were all about him.

There was a photo of Stilton when he received the Ratitzer Prize, the most important literary award on Mouse Island.

The back wall was covered with a giant photograph of . . . Can you guess who?

That's right! It was his beloved goldfish, **Hannibal**.

Stilton's desk, which is made of beautiful cherrywood, has five drawers. We inspected the desk immediately.

1. In the first drawer, we found a photograph of the **STILTON FAMILY**, with an inscription from his nephew Benjamin. *(We've concluded that Geronimo is well loved by his family!)*

2. In the second drawer, we found notes and **dozens and dozens of pens** with the names of hotels from all over the world printed on them. *(We've concluded that even though he has a computer, he still likes to write by hand!)*

Geronimo with his Ratitzer Prize

3. In the third drawer, we found his chock-full address book along with his precious journal: It was very messy-looking, with pieces of paper sticking out all over the place. *(We've concluded that he has a ton of friends, and that he's a real chatterbox!)*

4. In the fourth drawer, we found an assortment of BANDAGES and all kinds of medicine. *(We've concluded that he's afraid of getting sick!)*

5. The fifth and last drawer was LOCKED, but we managed to open it all the same. And we couldn't believe our eyes. It was full of . . .

CHEESE RINDS!

(We've concluded that he's a serious food lover, and that he constantly nibbles on cheese while he works!)

CHATTER

Super Scoop!

The editor of The Rodent's Gazette never misses an episode of Days of Our Mice!

We've caught Geronimo with a television hidden in his desk drawer! Even while he's working, he won't miss a minute of his favorite soap opera, *Days of Our Mice!*

CAN IT BE TRUE?

NO ONE'S PERFECT!

by Samantha Tattletail

I knew this book wouldn't be complete without an interview with the mouse himself, *Geronimo Stilton*!

So I went back to *The Rodent's Gazette* — during the day this time!

Geronimo asked me to sit down, offered me a cup of **hot chocolate** and some cheese snacks, and politely asked what he could do for me.

What can I do for you?

Well, I must admit that what everyone says is true: *Geronimo Stilton* is a true *gentlemouse*!

So I began the **interview**.

Samantha: Mr. Stilton, I've written a book . . . .

Geronimo: Oh, really? A book? How interesting! What is it about?

Samantha: Um . . . it's about . . . **you**.

Geronimo: Really? A book about me? Well, I'm not sure that's a very **interesting** subject. . . .

Samantha: Of course it is! Thousands, no, millions of readers want to know everything about you: what you like to eat, what your office is like, what you were like as a **CHiLD** . . .

Geronimo: **Ha, ha, ha!** Well, if my readers want to know everything about me, then it's a good thing you've written this book.

Samantha: So . . . you're not upset that I wrote it?

Geronimo:

Absolutely not!

Samantha: But some of your friends may have spilled a few of your secrets in the book.

Geronimo: I don't have anything to keep secret. In fact, if you have any questions for me, I'd be happy to answer them! I *love* my readers, and I'm HAPPY to let them know everything about me! I have plenty of faults, as you can tell, but no one's perfect, right?

We shook paws and repeated together:

"No one's perfect!"

But the interview wasn't quite over yet.

Samantha: Mr. Stilton, I do have one question I've been dying to ask. . . .

Geronimo settled into his chair, poured himself another cup of **hot chocolate** and filled his bowl with many, many more cheese snacks. Then he cleared his throat and said:

"Well, what would you like to know?"

THE TRUE STORY OF GERONIMO STILTON

by Samantha Tattletail

Samantha: I can tell from my interviews with your friends and family that in spite of your **FAULTS**, you're certainly a very **SPECIAL** rodent. But . . .

Geronimo: **BUT???**

Samantha: But I'm still **curious** about one thing. With the help of **Simon Squealer**, I've discovered all kinds of things about you, even

What's your real story?

I'll tell you!

28

what's in your desk drawers here in the office! But I still don't know anything about where you come from!

Geronimo: Ah, you've asked me a very important question. And I will GLADLY answer it.

How EXCITING! This was an **exclusive**! I paid close attention and took notes. . . .

Samantha: Really? This is important news! It's a real **scoop**!

Geronimo: I'm happy to tell you my real story. It is truly marvelous, like all stories about *love*!

Samantha: And I'm happy to hear it!

Geronimo: Well, you see, I don't know my actual parents. When I was very **young**, I was adopted by the **STILTON FAMILY**. Aunt Sweetfur, Grandfather William Shortpaws, Grandma Rose, Aunt Stitchy, Uncle Kindpaws, and all the others very **lovingly** adopted me. From that moment, the **STILTON FAMILY** has been my real family! This is why when people ask me who I am, I **always** reply: My name is Stilton, *Geronimo Stilton*! I'm proud to bear the name of the family that L♥VES me so dearly!

WILLIAM SHORTPAWS

AUNT SWEETFUR

TRAP STILTON

AUNT STITCHY

Just at that moment, someone knocked on the door to Geronimo's office. In came Thea, Trap, William Shortpaws, and Aunt Sweetfur, who were stopping by to say hello to Geronimo!

He looked at me, then jumped up and hugged them **tightly**. "True love has no limits. People who may have been born far apart can become **close** because they love each other!"

And that, dear readers, is the true story of *Geronimo Stilton*!

UNCLE GRAYFUR

GRANDMA ROSE

UNCLE KINDPAWS

THEA STILTON

Dear mouse friends,
Thanks for reading, and farewell
till the next book.

Geronimo Stilton